Michael Dahl

Richard Pellegrino

Raint

www.raintreepublishers.co.uk

Visit our website to find out
more information about
Raintree books.

To order:

Phone 0845 6044371
Fax +44 (0) 1865 312263
Email myorders@capstonepub.co.uk

Customers from outside the UK please telephone +44 1865 312262

Raintree is an imprint of Capstone Global Library
Limited, a company incorporated in England and Wales
having its registered office at 7 Pilgrim Street, London,
EC4V 6LB – Registered company number: 6695582

"Raintree" is a registered trademark
of Pearson Education Limited, under licence
to Capstone Global Library Limited

Text © Stone Arch Books 2009
First published in the United Kingdom in hardback
and paperback by Capstone Global Library in 2010
The moral rights of the proprietor have been asserted

Creative Director: Heather Kindseth
Graphic Designer: Brann Garvey
UK Editor: Vaarunika Dharmapala
Originated by Capstone Global Library Ltd
Printed and bound in China by South China
Printing Company Ltd

ISBN 978 1 406215 14 4 (hardback)
14 13 12 11 10
10 9 8 7 6 5 4 3 2 1

ISBN 978 1 406215 28 1 (paperback)
14 13 12 11 10
10 9 8 7 6 5 4 3 2 1

British Library Cataloguing in Publication Data
A full catalogue record for this book is available from
the British Library.

CONTENTS

Introduction

A new **Age of Dragons** is about to begin. The **powerful** creatures will return to rule the **world** once more, but this time it will be **different**. This time, they will have allies who will **help** them. Around the world, some young humans are making a strange **discovery**. They are learning that they were born with **dragon blood** – blood that gives them **amazing powers**.

CHAPTER 1
The Stowaway

A cargo ship moved across the Atlantic Ocean.

Dark clouds filled the sky.

Dark waves slapped against the ship's metal hull.

Eli hid on the ship. He was a stowaway.

Quietly, Eli stepped out from his hiding place.

A man's hand reached out from the darkness and grabbed Eli's arm.

CHAPTER 2
The Tattoo

9

"What are you doing here?" growled the older man. He was a sailor on the ship.

Eli froze. "I want to go to America," he said. "I want to work. I want a new life."

The man stared hard at Eli.

"Don't worry," the man said. "I understand."

Eli stared at the man's arm.

The skin was covered with a wild,

colourful tattoo.

It was a flying **dragon.**

The man looked around to
make sure no one was watching.

Then he said, "Come with me. We need to get you something to eat."

Eli relaxed. Then he followed the man through a storeroom.

He felt grateful to the older man. He was also confused.

The dragon tattoo reminded him of something.

The man's tattoo looked like the birthmark Eli had on his own arm.

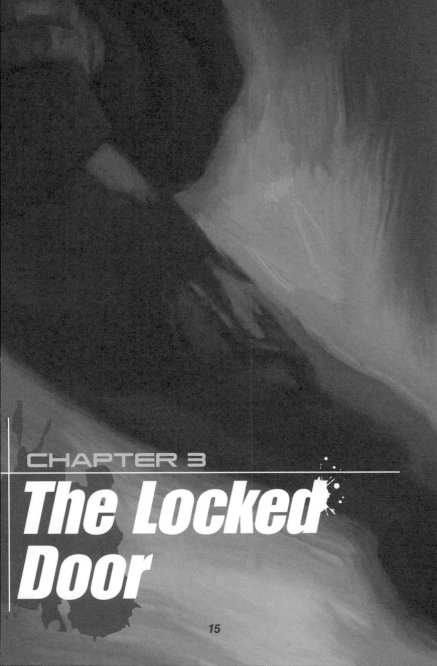

CHAPTER 3
The Locked Door

The sailor led Eli below the ship's decks.

They walked down several sets of metal stairs.

Eli could feel the ship move when the dark waves slapped against its side.

They passed a metal door. There was a sign on the door. It read: Cargo Room.

The man turned to Eli and said, "That room is off limits. No one goes in there but the captain."

Eli passed by the door.

His arm felt strange. The birthmark felt as if it was burning his skin.

When the door was behind him,

the burning feeling went away.

CHAPTER 4
A Trick?

Inside a room, the sailor gave Eli a bowl of soup.

"I know what it's like to leave your home behind," said the man. "I wanted a new life too."

"Just make sure no one sees you," he warned Eli. "I'll get you off the ship when we reach port."

Eli slept in a bunk above the man's bed.

In the middle of the night, a noise woke him up.

The man was leaving the cabin.

As soon as the door closed, Eli jumped out of his bunk.

He wondered if the man had tricked him.

Would the man bring the captain? Would they arrest Eli for hiding on the ship?

Eli left the cabin. He hurried back towards the metal steps.

Suddenly, he stopped.

The sailor was walking through
the door marked **Cargo Room.**

"What's he doing?" Eli

whispered.

CHAPTER 5
Secret Cargo

Eli followed the man into the forbidden room. His birthmark began to burn again.

Deep inside the dark room, Eli saw the man.

The man was staring at open wooden boxes.

He raised his arms above his head and shouted, "NO!"

The wooden boxes were full of eggs.

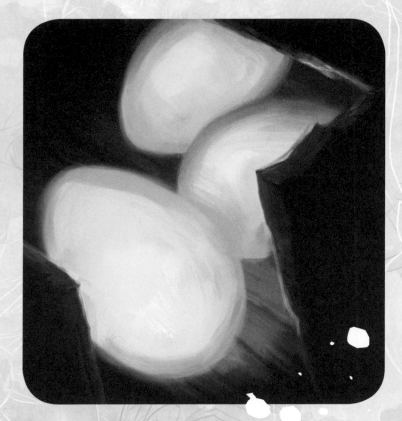

Gigantic eggs!

"These do not belong to humans!" cried the man. "They should be free!"

Eli felt a warm breeze. A flash of light blinded him.

Then he blinked his eyes. The man had changed. Instead of a man standing in the darkness, there was a dragon with wings.

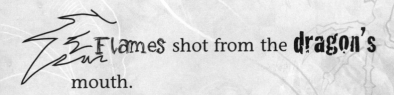 **Flames** shot from the **dragon's** mouth.

The flames melted the metal wall of the room. Eli could see the night sky through the opening.

Then the **dragon** flapped its wings.

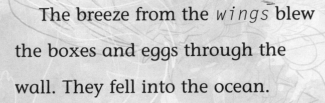

The breeze from the *wings* blew the boxes and eggs through the wall. They fell into the ocean.

The dragon turned and looked at Eli. It flashed its teeth.

"You are one of us," growled the dragon.

Spreading its wings, the dragon flew through the opening and was gone.

"Who are you?" yelled Eli.

Eli's birthmark suddenly felt like *ice*.

Colour began to seep into the edges of the birthmark. Now it looked even more like the man's **dragon** tattoo.

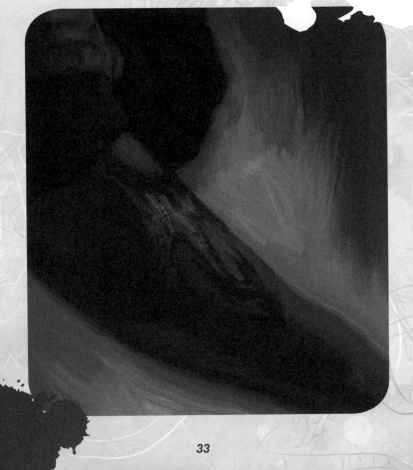

Of Dragons and Near-Dragons

Reptile eggs are always white to begin with. Many reptile eggs are rubbery. The eggs of turtles, geckos, and some other species are hard. The eggs of snakes and most lizards are softer and feel like leather.

Most reptiles lay eggs. However, some species of reptiles deliver live young.

In the species that lay eggs, the female digs a hole. She puts the eggs into the hole and buries them. This helps protect the eggs from predators.

In the wild, reptile eggs are usually buried. In captivity, eggs are placed in an incubator. This machine keeps eggs warm until they hatch.

Reptile eggs have many predators, including other reptiles. The African egg-eating snake will swallow another egg whole. Then it cracks the egg open and swallows the contents. In the end, it will spit out the egg shell in one piece.

The leatherback turtle is the world's largest reptile. Females can lay as many as 1,000 eggs in one season!

ABOUT THE AUTHOR

Michael Dahl is the author of more than 200 books for children and young adults. He has won the AEP Distinguished Achievement Award three times for his non-fiction. His *Finnegan Zwake* mystery series was shortlisted twice by the Anthony and Agatha awards. He has also written the *Library of Doom* series. He is a featured speaker at conferences around the country on graphic novels and high-interest books for boys.

ABOUT THE ILLUSTRATOR

Richard Pellegrino is a professional illustrator. His work has been published by CMYK, Night Shade Books, Compass Press, and Tale Bones Press. He is also an accomplished figurative painter and has shown his oil paintings in numerous galleries.

GLOSSARY

allies people or countries that give support to each other

birthmark mark on the skin that was there from birth

creature living thing that is human or animal

forbidden when something is off limits or entry is not allowed

grateful thankful and appreciative

hull frame or body of a boat or ship

rule have power over something

seep flow or trickle slowly

stowaway someone who hides in a plane, ship, or boat to avoid paying for the trip

DISCUSSION QUESTIONS

1. Do you think it was right for Eli to sneak on to the cargo ship? Why or why not?

2. Why did Eli's arm burn when he walked by the cargo room?

3. Why do you think the old man was nice to Eli right away?

WRITING PROMPTS

1. Do you think the old man was a good or bad person? Write a paragraph explaining your answer.

2. Were you surprised by the ending? Write a paragraph explaining your answer.

3. What do you think happens to Eli after the dragon flies away? Write another chapter to the story. Be sure to include what happens to the old man too.

MORE BOOKS TO READ

LIBRARY OF DOOM

Meet the mysterious Librarian. Keeper of the world's most dangerous books, sworn enemy of monsters made of paper and ink, crusader of young people threatened by ancient curses... Enter the Library of Doom to follow these heart-pounding adventures.

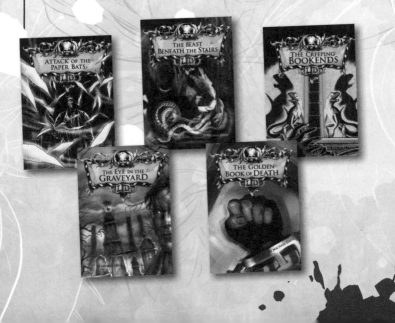